A Snowgirl named just Sue

This story is dedicated to everyone who believes
in the amazing power of positive thinking.
Together we really can make the world a better place!
—Mark

To all those who believed in Bob.
—Karen

A Snowgirl named just Sue

Written by
Mark Kimball Moulton

Illustrated by Karen Hillard Good

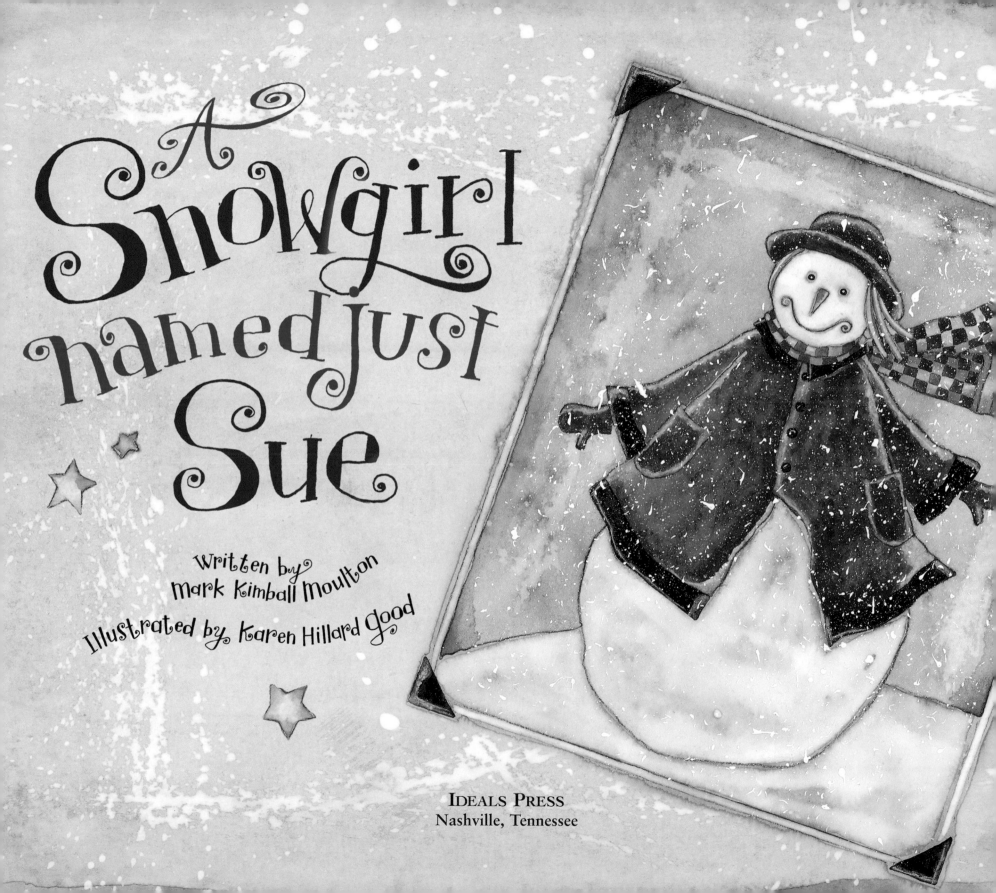

IDEALS PRESS
Nashville, Tennessee

ISBN 0-8249-5150-6

Published by Ideals Press
An imprint of Ideals Publications
A division of Guideposts
535 Metroplex Drive, Suite 250
Nashville, Tennessee 37211
www.idealsbooks.com

Color separations by Precision Color Graphics, Franklin, Wisconsin

Printed and bound in Italy by LEGO

Library of Congress Cataloging-in-Publication Data

Moulton, Mark Kimball.
 A snowgirl named Just Sue / written by Mark Kimball Moulton ;
illustrated by Karen Hillard Good.
  p. cm.
 Summary: A magical change in the weather not only saves
Snowman Bob from melting, but also inspires his friends to build
a snowgirl to keep him company.
 ISBN 0-8249-5150-6 (alk. paper)
 [1. Snowmen—Fiction. 2. Friendship—Fiction. 3. Stories in rhyme.]
 I. Good, Karen Hillard, ill. II. Title.
 PZ8.3.M8622Sm 2005
 [E]—dc22

                    2005002488

        1 3 5 7 9 10 8 6 4 2

This book is for

_____

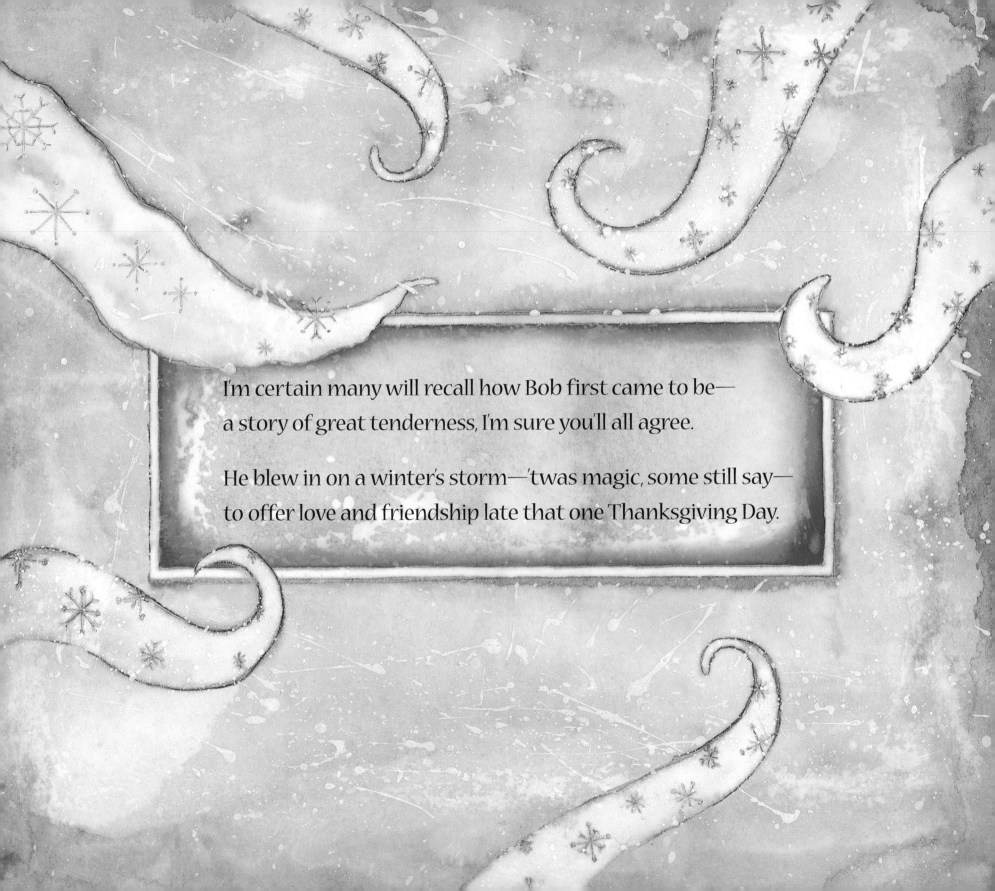

I'm certain many will recall how Bob first came to be—
a story of great tenderness, I'm sure you'll all agree.

He blew in on a winter's storm—'twas magic, some still say—
to offer love and friendship late that one Thanksgiving Day.

In the snow, I heard a whisper.
The voice was soft and kind.
He asked for my assistance and,
of course, I didn't mind.

I gathered up those many flakes
and rolled them in a ball,
so he could be, and be with me,
in shape and form and all.

Then, with the help of many hands,
we built our Snowman Bob.
And looking back, I'm proud to say
we did a right good job!

Bob came to share a message,
an important one to know—
that friends may come in many forms,
some even made of snow!

We never will forget our friend, come rain or sunny weather.
We know that he will be with us—we'll always be together....

For Bob had shared another thought:
"Good friends are always near,
as long as they're remembered in your heart throughout the year!"

I wonder, though, how many folks know of our other visit.
The time we met a friend of Bob's—it isn't well known, is it?

Well, gather round me now, my friends, and I will gladly share
the tale of how we helped our friend find love *extraordinaire!*

'Twas early February;
all the holidays had passed.
Christmas, Kwanzaa, Hanukkah—
each one had been a blast!

The weather had remained quite cold,
and Snowman Bob still stood
exactly where we'd built our friend.
And, gee, he still looked good!

There'd been a few warm, sunny days.
He'd lost a pound or two.
But, all in all, we thought our friend
looked just as good as new.

Oh, yes, we'd had tremendous fun
with Snowman Bob that year.
He'd filled our days with happiness,
good friendship, and good cheer.

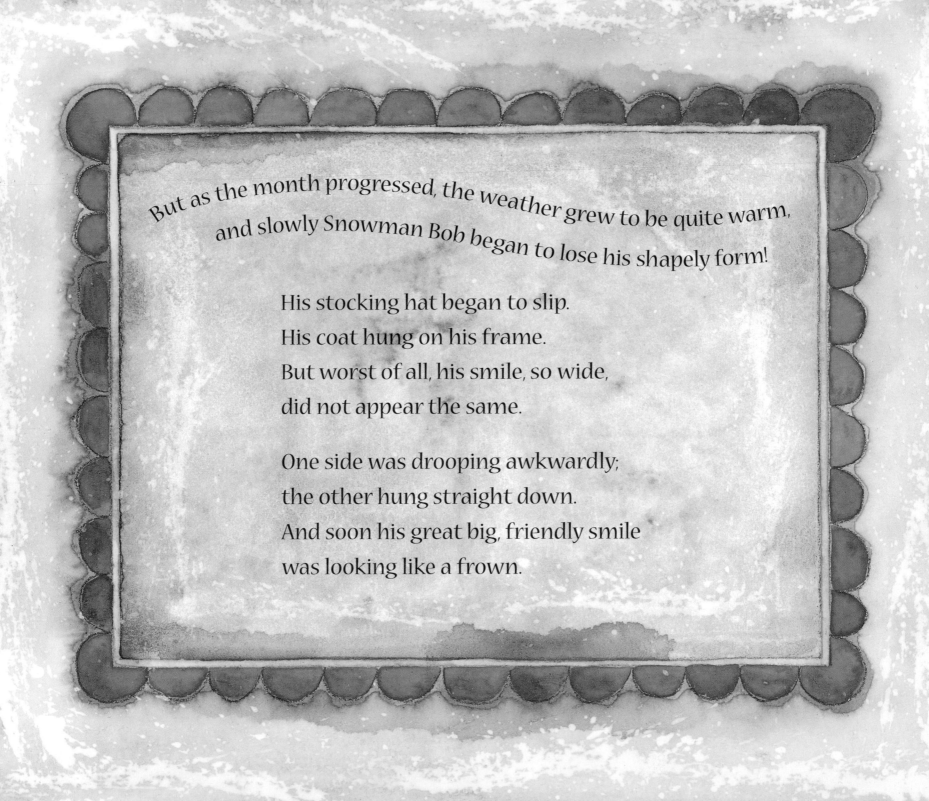

But as the month progressed, the weather grew to be quite warm,
and slowly Snowman Bob began to lose his shapely form!

His stocking hat began to slip.
His coat hung on his frame.
But worst of all, his smile, so wide,
did not appear the same.

One side was drooping awkwardly;
the other hung straight down.
And soon his great big, friendly smile
was looking like a frown.

My friends and family gathered round,
not knowing what to do—
we knew that it was up to us
to help our friend get through.

But, frankly, we had no idea
of how to help our friend.
Then just like last Thanksgiving,
magic visited again!

The weatherman reported only rain was due that night,
but we all wished that it would snow—we wished with all our might!

And as we wished and hoped and prayed, the clouds came rolling in,
obscuring all the twinkles in the sky where stars had been.

LOCAL WEATHER
Rain
80% chance

It took awhile, but, sure enough, one tiny raindrop fell.
And we began to wonder, "Should we bid our Bob farewell?"

Just when it seemed the rain would fall
and wash away our dreams,
Sir Moon appeared and took a bow
and shed his softest beams.

And this is when, I dare to say,
that magic came again,
as I stood there beneath the moon
with family and friends.

For suddenly the wind began to dance among the trees;
and, sure enough, we felt the temperature begin to freeze!

And with a nod, Sir Moon stood back and gave us each a smile.
Then instantly the sky was filled with snow for miles and miles.

We blinked to clear our vision, gave a cheer, and clapped our hands,
spun round and round in circles until we could barely stand!

The snow began to spiral, then to lightly settle down,
as it began to blanket every inch of our small town.

Snow frosted all our neighbors' homes, like icing on a cake,
and every flake was different—every tiny, little flake.

Snow landed on our windowsills.
It landed in our hair.
It spread a cloak of peace and love
and beauty everywhere.

And while we watched, enchanted
by the wonder of it all,
we saw the slightest shimmer
in that magical snowfall.

The snow took on an eerie cast—
first pink, then red, then rose.
Then goose bumps started running
from our heads down to our toes.

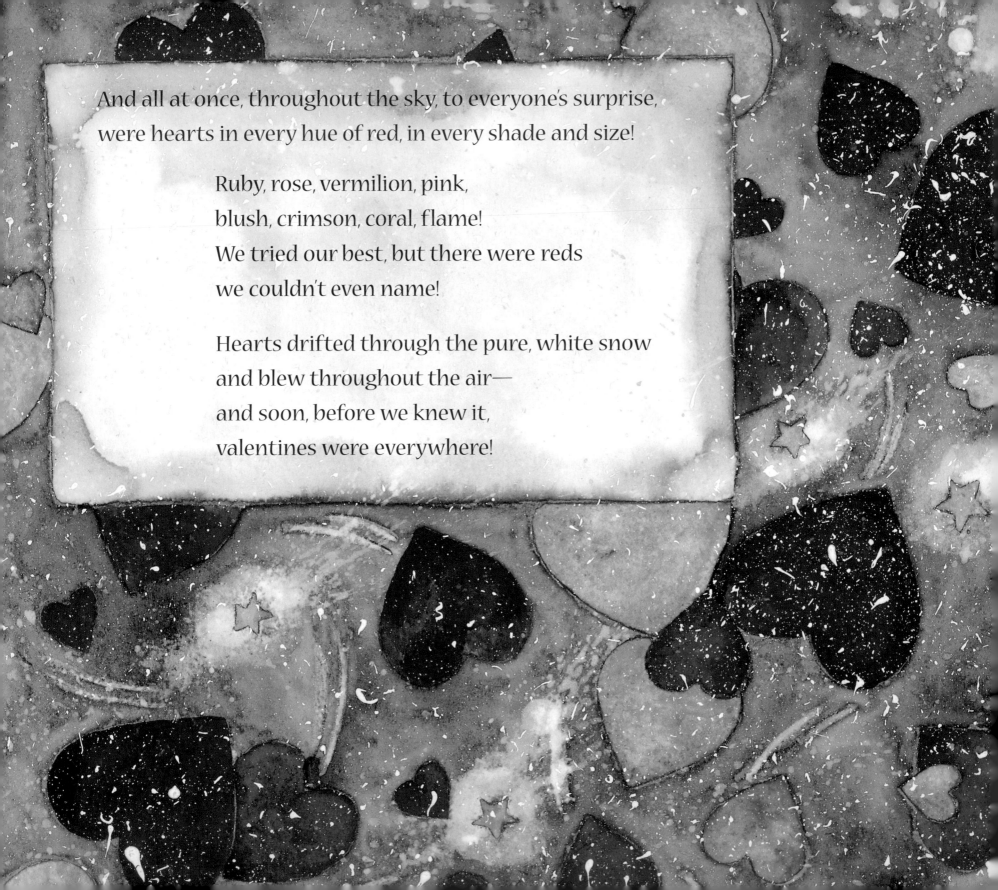

And all at once, throughout the sky, to everyone's surprise,
were hearts in every hue of red, in every shade and size!

Ruby, rose, vermilion, pink,
blush, crimson, coral, flame!
We tried our best, but there were reds
we couldn't even name!

Hearts drifted through the pure, white snow
and blew throughout the air—
and soon, before we knew it,
valentines were everywhere!

They landed on the rooftops and
on all the walks and streets,
on all our pets—our dogs and cats,
even our parakeets!

On every car and bike and sled
were heart-shaped valentines.
Each card had lace-lined edges and
the simple words, "Be Mine."

Red hearts were perched in every tree,
on every evergreen.
It was the most amazing sight
that you have ever seen!

'Twas then that we all realized
just what we had to do.
We had to build a friend for Bob—
a snowgirl named just "Sue."

We danced and sang and ran about
as Sue began to be.
And if I do say so myself,
she turned out heavenly!

Some coal for eyes, a mop for hair,
some sticks, a wide-brimmed hat,
the sweetest smile you've ever seen,
a coat, and that was that!

We joined in celebration, singing songs and having fun, so pleased with one another for another job well done.

But soon we all grew hungry,
and our cheeks were red as beets.
So off we ran to Mother's house
to have a bite to eat.

Now, perhaps you may be thinking
that magic ruled that day,
but this will seem like nothing
compared to what was on its way.

For after we'd had cocoa and
returned a little later,
it seemed to us our Snowman Bob
stood just a little straighter.

And in his coal-black eyes there now
appeared a merry gleam
that made him look contented,
like a kitty lapping cream.

The smile that once appeared to be
a long, lopsided frown
now stretched across his face just like
a silly circus clown's.

But what was most unusual, what really was *most* grand
was now our new friends, Bob and Sue, were standing holding hands!

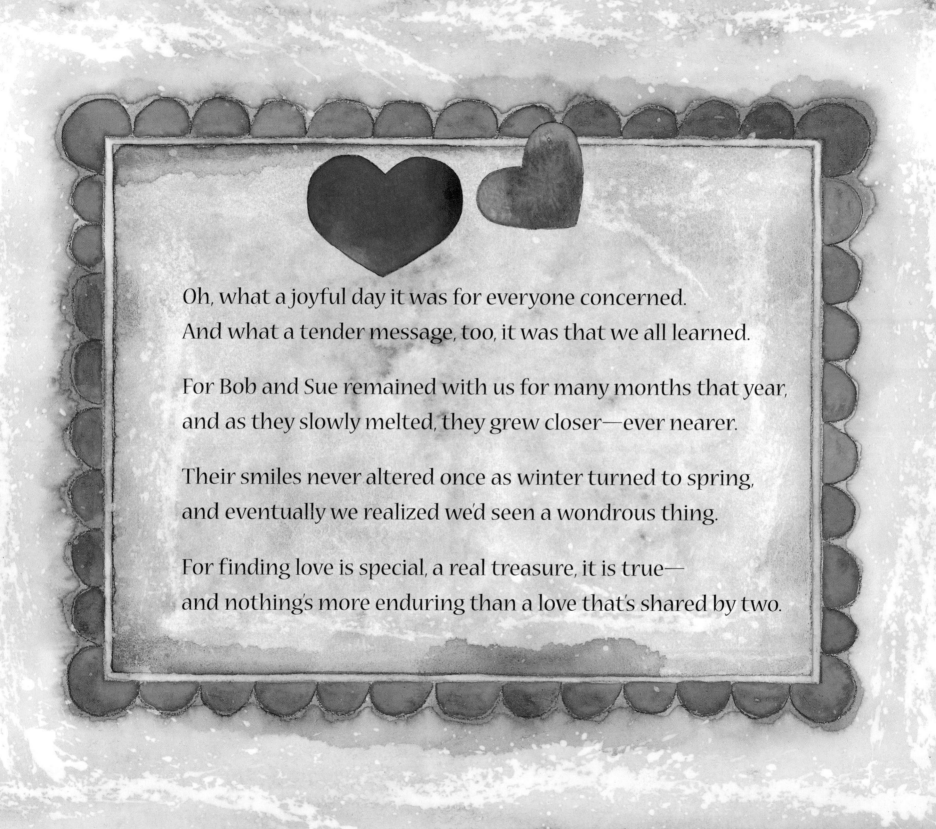

Oh, what a joyful day it was for everyone concerned.
And what a tender message, too, it was that we all learned.

For Bob and Sue remained with us for many months that year,
and as they slowly melted, they grew closer—ever nearer.

Their smiles never altered once as winter turned to spring,
and eventually we realized we'd seen a wondrous thing.

For finding love is special, a real treasure, it is true—
and nothing's more enduring than a love that's shared by two.

Although we've reached the ending of this story, never fear;
for could that be the laughter of snow-children that we hear?